ALSO BY ELISE GRAVEL

ELISE GRAVEL

OLGA

OUT OF CONTROL!

HARPER
An Imprint of HarperCollinsPublishers

To Jill Davis,
Olga's other mom

Welcome to my latest notebook. My name is Olga. You might be familiar with me since I'm the kid who discovered a fascinating new animal species:

THE OLGAMUS RIDICULUS.

Here's what I know about her so far:

1. SHE LIKES TO **SLEEP** IN A **GARBAGE CAN.**

2. SHE SMELLS **BAD.**

3. SHE **LOVES** TO **CUDDLE.**

4. SHE **ONLY** EATS **OLIVES.**

5. SHE'S **NICER** THAN MOST **HUMANS.**

ANNOYING HUMANS

My specimen is an adorable female that I named Meh because of the sound she makes all the time.

I used to be a lonely kid. My only friend was my spider, Rita, who lives under the sink.

RITA THE SPIDER

SALUT*

*SHE SPEAKS ONLY FRENCH.

But since I discovered Meh, my life has changed for the better.

I used to think that animals were the only friends I would ever make. I made this bar graph to compare my feelings for humans and animals. Not hard to guess who the winner is!

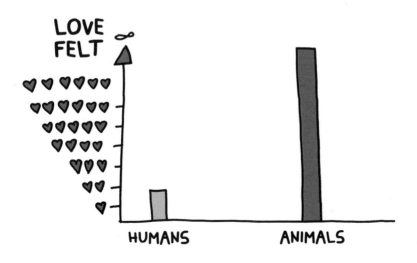

LOVE FELT

HUMANS   ANIMALS

I still think that animals are way cooler than humans. If I was given the chance to redesign the human body, I'd give us more animal features.

WINGS

FANGS

SCALES

WEBBED FEET

LONG **FLUFFY** TAILS

NIGHT VISION

SONAR

RETRACTABLE **CLAWS**

Because of Meh I began to go out and meet interesting humans. She gave a purpose to my life.

MY LIFE BEFORE MEH:

GRUMPY

MY **ONLY** FRIEND

MY LIFE WITH MEH:

MS. SWOOP

MR. HOOPAH

CHUCK

THE LALAS

MISTER

Life with Meh is chock-full of amazing discoveries, but the latest one is by far the biggest. I opened my fridge yesterday to find her snuggled among a bunch of

BABY OLGAMUSES!

Seven of them, to be precise.

I don't know about you, but finding seven baby *Olgamus*es in my fridge is not something that happens to me every day!

OTHER THINGS
THAT DON'T HAPPEN TO ME
EVERY DAY:

RIDING A
RHINO

SEEING A
FLYING GRANDMA

WANT A PEPPERMINT, SWEETIE?

FINDING A **$100** BILL
IN MY **OWN EAR**

I think I could say without exaggerating that yester-day was the most exciting (and exhausting) day of my life.

SEVEN BABY OLGAMUSES!

And they were  **SO CUTE!**

So delicate, so tiny, so weird looking! How I itched to pick one up to look at it more closely, but when I got my hand too close to them, Meh didn't like it one bit.

DOWDOWDOW!

SHH, IT'S OKAY, MEH.

OBSERVATION #1:

MAMA *OLGAMUSES* DON'T LIKE IT WHEN WE TRY TO TOUCH THEIR BABIES.

Some of my friends were at my house with me when I discovered the babies. They were as fascinated as I was.

We spent a few minutes watching them quietly. Then one of my friends, Farla, got a funny look on her face and screamed:

I call Farla and her sister, Shalala, the Lalas. They're sort of my frenemies, and they have a tendency to notice yucky things and are easily disgusted. I find this annoying, but I guess they have other good qualities.

Plus, they were right about the fridge. It was HORRIFYING.

I'm not very good at cleaning. Like many scientists, I'm very busy with my research, and sometimes cleaning ends up at the bottom of my priority list. Anyway, my fridge is usually pretty empty. Yesterday, though, it was not.

It was cleanup time, all right. We got rid of a bunch of junk, wiped down the glass shelves using some Windex and a sponge, and cleared a whole shelf out for Meh and the babies.

THE CLEANING SQUAD!

Chuck came back with the dog bed that Mister used as a baby.

I didn't want to pick the babies up and disturb the little family, so I gently closed the fridge door and waited to see if Meh would transfer her babies to the cozy shelf.

"COZY" AND "FRIDGE" ARE
NOT FREQUENTLY USED TOGETHER
IN THE SAME SENTENCE.

While we waited, I opened my notebook and wrote down four OBSERVATIONS:

OBSERVATION # 3:

BABY *OLGAMUSES* NEED A **COLD** ENVIRONMENT.

THEIR SKIN IS **TRANSLUCENT,** SO WE CAN SEE THEIR **ORGANS.**

THEY SEEM TO **NURSE** LIKE **KITTENS** OR **PUPPIES,** BUT I'M **NOT SURE.**

MAMA *OLGAMUSES* ARE **VERY PROTECTIVE** OF THEIR **BABIES.**

DOWDOWDOW!

This notebook is going to fill up pretty quickly! Oh, how I wish I could see right through the fridge door! I'd just spend every minute looking at the babies.

Any excuse to go to Mr. Hoopah's store is good. I love
that place.

What I've found recently at

MR. HOOPAH'S STORE:

 REAL LIVE
CARNIVOROUS
PLANTS

 CANNED
ACORN
SOUP

 CHICKEN BROTH
FRAGRANCE

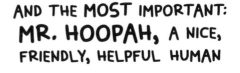 CHICKEN-
SHAPED
LAMPS

 EDIBLE
FORKS AND
SPOONS

AND THE MOST IMPORTANT:
MR. HOOPAH, A NICE,
FRIENDLY, HELPFUL HUMAN

HOW CAN I HELP YOU TODAY,
LOYAL CUSTOMERS?*

*MR. HOOPAH IS **ALWAYS** VERY FORMAL.

We told him about the baby *Olgamuse*s. He was very excited.

Mr. Hoopah disappeared into the back of the store, which seems like the most mysterious place. It must be full of treasures like Ali Baba's cave. I sometimes wonder if he lives there.

He came back quickly carrying a giant jar. He looked very proud.

I thanked him and took the jar, and we were about to leave when I felt my stomach grumble. Chuck, the Lalas, and I looked around for interesting snacks. Here were some of our choices:

MARINATED
PINECONE
HEARTS

SMOKED-OYSTER
MUFFINS

MANGO AND HAM
POPSICLES

VEGETARIAN
CHICKEN WINGS

MAC-AND-CHEESE-FLAVORED
INSTANT **RAMEN** SOUP

FRIED JELLYFISH
CHIPS

Of course, I went for the mac-and-cheese-flavored ramen. The others picked their own snacks (fried jellyfish chips for Shalala, crab cakes for Farla, and vegetarian chicken wings for Chuck), and then Farla asked me if I wanted to go sit at the picnic table outside the store with them.

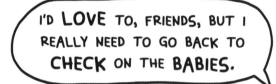

I'D **LOVE** TO, FRIENDS, BUT I REALLY NEED TO GO BACK TO **CHECK** ON THE **BABIES**.

At home, I set my snack down on the table, washed my hands, and opened the fridge door to take one last look at the babies before going to bed. They were quiet, half asleep, and so was Meh.

I played them a little lullaby on the ukulele that I composed on the spot. I felt very inspired.

Then I went to sleep right next to the fridge, on the floor. I had totally forgotten to eat my mac and cheese.

OBSERVATION #4:

TAKING CARE OF NEWBORNS WILL MAKE
A GAL FORGET ABOUT HER OWN NEEDS.

I woke up early in the morning and cleaned up the rest
of the kitchen as best as I could. From what I know,
newborns are vulnerable to infections and viruses.
Their environment has to be kept clean.

MEET THE NEW OLGA, THE SQUEAKY-CLEAN QUEEN!*

*FUN GAME: TRY TO SAY THAT 10 TIMES QUICKLY.

Normally, I would hate doing all this cleaning, but I didn't mind. Why? Because it was

FOR THE GOOD OF THE BABIES.

★ ★★★ ★ ★★★ ★★★

At around eight a.m., Meh called to me from inside the fridge. I opened the door, and she jumped out.

Meh ran to her food bowl and started wolfing down her olives. She seemed to enjoy the bacon-wrapped olives as much as Mr. Hoopah thought she would.

MEH'S VERY ELEGANT EATING STYLE

While she was eating, I took a look at the babies. They were all squirming around. Without Meh right there, it was easier to get a closer look.

I will draw them here so you can take a look too:

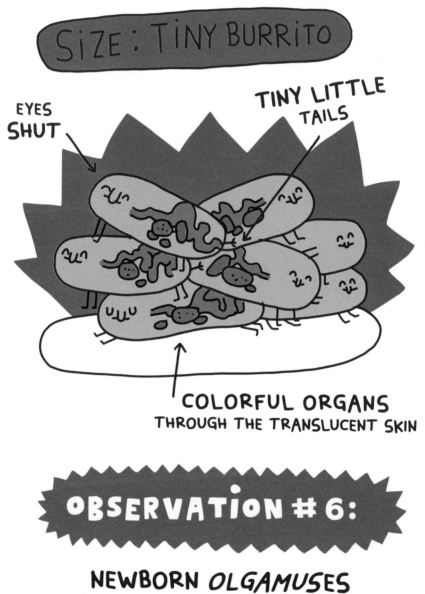

SIZE: TINY BURRITO

EYES SHUT

TINY LITTLE TAILS

COLORFUL ORGANS
THROUGH THE TRANSLUCENT SKIN

OBSERVATION #6:

NEWBORN *OLGAMUSES*
ALL LOOK THE SAME!

Meh came back and sat next to me for a minute. I took some time to pet her, hug her, and tell her how proud I was of her big accomplishment. After all, giving birth is a huge deal!

She was quickly shedding her extra pregnancy weight, but she still looked tired.

MEH BEFORE
GIVING BIRTH

MEH **AFTER**
GIVING BIRTH

She hopped back on the shelf, snuggled with her babies, and started making her purring sound again. She sounded a little bit like a dishwasher. She looked so happy and so proud. I took a photo on my phone.

PROUD MAMA

I closed the fridge door to let the new family have a rest. But then I didn't know what to do next. I felt a bit restless.

So I kept myself busy by writing down a few observations I'd come up with:

OBSERVATION # 7:

MEH CARRIES HER BABIES BY **GRABBING** THEM BY THEIR **SKINNY TAILS.**

THE BABIES' **FEEDING SCHEDULE:** THEY SEEM TO NURSE **ALL** THE TIME.

THE BABIES CAN'T **WALK.** THEY **CAN'T OPEN** THEIR EYES. AND THEY DON'T MAKE ANY **NOISE.**

COMPARATIVE CHART

•••••••••••••••••••••••••

	SPRING ROLLS	BABY *OLGAMUS*
CUTENESS	X	XXX
TASTE	XXX	NO DATA
LEVEL OF ENERGY	O	O
SMELL	YUMMY	NOT YUMMY
SIZE	TINY BURRITO	TINY BURRITO

I spent the rest of the evening feeding Rita dead flies I found on the windowsill. I like Rita, but she's not the most talkative companion. (Sorry, Rita)

I can't wait until the babies get a little

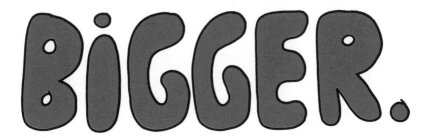

3

MINI PLANETS

Cleaning water bowls is fine, but I wanted to find a more helpful way to support Meh in her new life. Of course, I couldn't nurse the babies, so I felt useless.

There is one thing I do really well, and that is RESEARCH. I mean, there are other things I do well, too, like:

But I'm not sure these skills would help Meh much.

I decided to go to the library and get some books about how to take care of newborns. Sure, I could always do research online on my computer, but I really like the library because it has:

NEW COMIC BOOKS

PEACE AND QUIET

And above all, my friend Ms. Swoop, the nicest librarian ever, was at her desk today.

Ms. Swoop and I found only one book from the grown-ups section:

"Hmm," she said. "We only have this book about caring for human babies. I was hoping to find a book about baby hamsters or golden retrievers, but we don't have any here."

I spent the whole afternoon studying everything there is to know about human newborns. There was nothing in there about caring for animal babies, but I still had a fun time reading it.

FUN FACTS ABOUT BABIES:

NEWBORN BABY HEADS ARE **ONE-FOURTH** OF THEIR TOTAL WEIGHT. IF **GROWN-UPS** HAD THE SAME PROPORTIONS AS **BABIES**, THEIR HEADS WOULD BE AS BIG AS **MICROWAVE OVENS.**

NEWBORNS HAVE MORE **BONES** THAN ADULTS. WHEN THEY **GROW,** SOME OF THOSE BONES **FUSE TOGETHER** TO MAKE LARGER BONES.

MUTANT BONE

IN THE WOMB, BABIES ARE ENTIRELY **COVERED IN HAIR.**

IN THE WOMB, THEY **DRINK** THEIR OWN **PEE.**

NEWBORN BABIES CAN **HOLD THEIR BREATH UNDER WATER.***

IF BABIES' **GROWTH RATE** CONTINUED AT THE SAME RATE AS THEIR FIRST YEAR, THEY WOULD BE **GIANTS** BY THE TIME THEY BECAME **ADULTS.**

MY, MY, YOU'VE **GROWN** SO MUCH!

***DON'T** TRY THIS AT HOME.

46

Of course, none of this has anything to do with baby *Olgamuses*. I still found good basic info in there that I'll be able to apply to my new little pals.

WHAT NEWBORN MAMMALS NEED:

MILK

SAFETY

LOVE + CUDDLES

WARMTH

At this stage, Mama Meh is pretty much the only thing her babies need.

Then the doorbell rang. It was Chuck.

HEY! HOW ARE THE **BABIES** AND THE **MOM**?

THEY'RE **FINE!** THEY **SLEEP** ALL THE TIME.

He looked at the babies for a while. They were nursing. Mister sniffed at the babies, and Meh licked Mister on the nose.

LICK!

If Meh is an alien, she clearly comes from a planet that's not from our solar system. We would already know if life existed on a neighboring planet. So we looked for planets that have been discovered outside our solar neighborhood. They are called

EXOPLANETS.

There are hundreds of them!

Here's a list of seven exoplanets that would make cool names if we shorten them:

FULL NAME	NICKNAME
UPSILON ANDROMEDAE B	UPSI
MU ARAE C	MU
OGLE-2003-BLG-235LB	OGLE
POLLUX B	POLLUX
SWEEPS 04	SWEEPS
DENIS -P J082303.1-491201 B	DENIS
HD 142 B	HD142B (BECAUSE IT'S FUNNY)

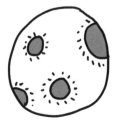

I love these names, but I guess we'd better wait till they grow a little bit to name them. Or how will we tell them apart?

OBSERVATION # 8:

THEY MIGHT BE:

IDENTICAL SEPTUPLETS!*

(I hope not!)

*Seven babies born at the same time from the same mother are called septuplets!

I'm sorry I skipped a whole week. So many things happened at the same time. I just didn't have a minute to myself!

OBSERVATION # 9:

BABIES ARE EXTREMELY

DEMANDING!

Here's what happened since I wrote my last entry:

THE BABIES ARE **GROWING** VERY FAST. THEY ARE NOW THE **SIZE** OF ADULT **GUINEA PIGS.**

MAMA MEH TOOK THEM **OUT** OF THE **FRIDGE** AND SET THEM UP IN HER OLD **TRASH CAN.** THEY'RE MUCH EASIER TO **OBSERVE** IN THERE.

THEY STARTED **WALKING**
(RUNNING, EVEN) AT **THREE**
DAYS, AND NOW THEY'RE
UNSTOPPABLE.

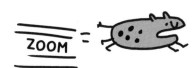

THEY STARTED SAYING **MEH**
WITH TINY LITTLE VOICES THAT
ARE **SO CUTE** IT MAKES ME
WANT TO **DROP** ON THE **FLOOR.**

THEY CAN NOW **OPEN** THEIR
BEAUTIFUL LITTLE BEADY **EYES.**

MAMA MEH LETS ME PICK
THEM UP NOW, SO I CAN
LOOK AT THEM
CLOSELY.

Here's a diagram of the inside of a baby *Olgamus*'s

BODY

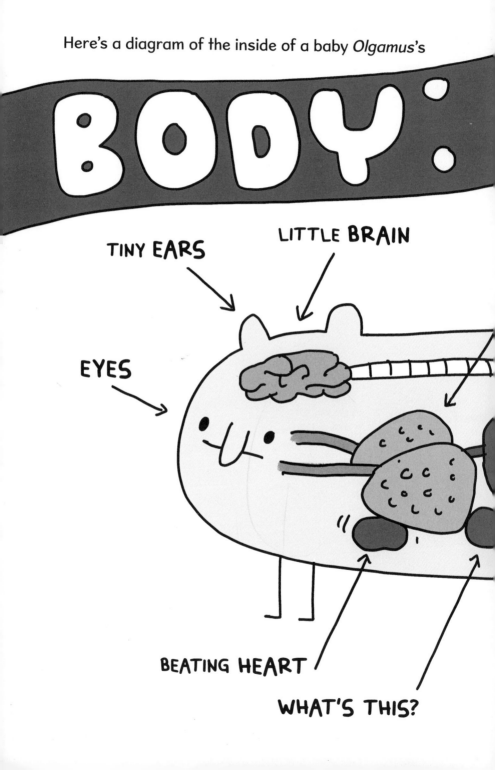

TINY EARS

LITTLE BRAIN

EYES

BEATING HEART

WHAT'S THIS?

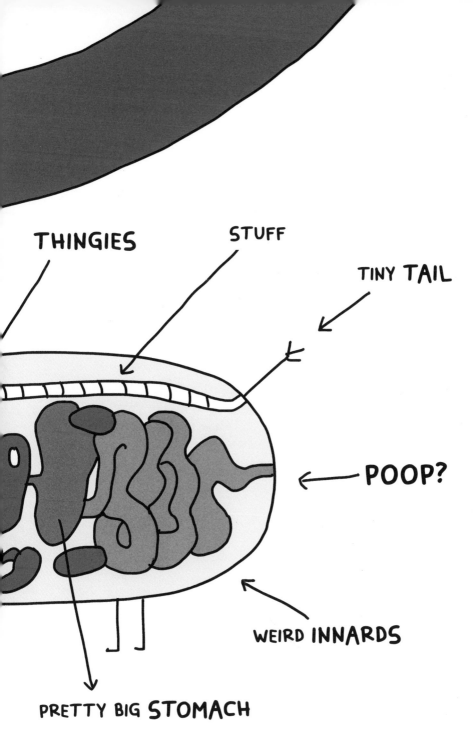

THINGIES

STUFF

TINY TAIL

POOP?

WEIRD INNARDS

PRETTY BIG STOMACH

WHOA!!!

They are starting to grow fur, so it won't be long until I can't see in there anymore. Each one looks slightly different, so I can finally tell them apart. Now I can name them:

UPSI

MU

OGLE

POLLUX

SWEEPS

DENIS

HD142B

They are all adorable, but look what they do!

I built a cage around Rita to protect her.

*LET ME **OUT!** I AM **INNOCENT!** (IN FRENCH)

At night, they won't let me sleep. They jump on my tummy and wake me up screaming at the top of their lungs:

Upsi is the biggest rascal. In just a few days, he's eaten two of my houseplants, peed on my computer keyboard, bitten Mister's tail, broken my lamp, and destroyed my favorite stuffed animal.

I like when the Lalas and Chuck come over to help me and babysit. I swear, without them, I'd be out of my mind.

This morning, they came to help me clean up. Sha-lala made some mac and cheese with pickles (my very favorite meal) because I never have time to make it myself. I really used to NOT LIKE these girls, but they are definitely growing on me.

65

*I AM THE ONLY *OLGAMUS* EXPERT ON EARTH.
I AM THE **BEST CAREGIVER** FOR THEIR SPECIES.

We tried to eat the mac and cheese while the babies were jumping on the table and climbing on our shoulders.

OBSERVATION # 10:

TRYING TO EAT WITH SEVEN *OLGAMUSES* IS AS HARD AS KNITTING IN A POOL FILLED WITH OVEREXCITED SEALS.

Then my phone rang.

This was great! Finally a chance to tell the world about my scientific discovery and my research!

Chuck and the Lalas wanted to know what the call was about. When I told them, I could tell the Lalas were impressed (and probably a bit jealous too). They love *Awesome* magazine.

"Will there be a photo shoot?" asked Farla.

"I guess so. *Awesome* magazine is 99 percent photos," I said. "They have pictures everywhere!"

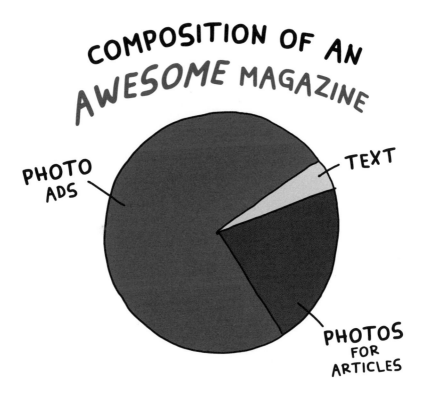

COMPOSITION OF AN AWESOME MAGAZINE

PHOTO ADS

TEXT

PHOTOS FOR ARTICLES

"EEEEEEE!!! Can we come? Can we come? Can we come?" asked Shalala. "We'll do your hair!"

Sigh. Again, they're only trying to help.

"Okay," I said. "See you tomorrow!"

After they all left, I sat down to watch them for a while. They all started to nurse ferociously. All but Mu, who was getting shoved away by his siblings.

They wouldn't let him in. Every time he got near a nipple, Upsi would shove him away, or Sweeps would bite his tail, or Denis would steal the nipple.

I felt bad for Mu. I have to make sure this isn't happening too much. I want all the babies to get enough to eat.

I'll have to keep an eye on the situation.

The people from *Awesome* magazine were here today.
It was exhausting and not exactly what I expected.

They came in the morning with their photographer
and spent about an hour putting stuff on my face and
doing crazy things with my hair.

THIS IS WHAT I LOOK LIKE WITH **TWO POUNDS** OF **GUNK** ON MY HEAD.

WHO IS THIS?

The Lalas were disappointed. They think they are THE beauty experts, but this time they just had to sit in the corner and watch the professionals.

After the makeup artists were done, the reporter introduced herself. Her name was Dorina Spirula. She looked very excited to see me. I went and got Meh and started telling her about the night I discovered her and what I've found out about the species since then, but—

77

I didn't like it one bit, but I guess a girl's got to do what a girl's got to do in the name of science, so I put on the dress. Then they made me sit on my red chair holding Meh, and they snapped away for what felt like the whole afternoon.

OBSERVATION #12:

NOW I UNDERSTAND WHY SUPERMODELS OFTEN LOOK **ANNOYED.**

I was relieved when it was over. Finally! We would get to the interview part! I went to get my first notebook to show Dorina Spirula, but when I came back, she was putting on her jacket and heading out the door.

And just like that, they were gone, leaving my house smelling like the perfume section of a department store.

I was soooo disappointed. They didn't let me talk about my research. AT ALL. It was like they weren't even interested!

The Lalas were way more excited about the whole thing than I was. They had spent their time taking pictures for their Instasnap accounts, and they showed me their favorites:

I changed back to my beloved dress and sat with Meh on the bed. She was not happy with her hair gel either. She was all sticky and looked miserable.

DON'T WORRY, MEH. WE'LL TAKE A **BATH** TONIGHT. THE UPSIDE IS THAT **EVERYBODY** WILL KNOW ABOUT YOU AND YOUR SPECIES. WE'LL SHOW **HUMANS** HOW MUCH ANIMALS CAN TEACH US.

MEH.

I hugged her and gave her a kiss, but when I got up, I saw something was spread out all over the living room rug!

RAINBOW POOP EVERYWHERE! AHH! It was rainbow poop from all the babies. The Lalas helped me clean up. The quantity of little rainbow pellets was phenomenal.*

*THAT MEANS THERE WAS **A LOT!**

OBSERVATION # 13:

IF WE COULD FIND A WAY TO PRODUCE **ENERGY** FROM *OLGAMUS* POOP, MY HOUSE WOULD BE AS PRODUCTIVE AS A **POWER PLANT.**

OLGAMUSES = POOPING MACHINES

It was lunchtime, so we went to Mr. Hoopah's store to get something to eat.

When Mr. Hoopah saw us, the look on his face reminded me that I was still wearing the makeup the *Awesome* magazine makeup crew had put on me. The crazy hairdo too!

MEET OLGA

THE GROUCHIEST CELEBRITY

The storeroom! I had always been curious about what treasures were hiding in there. Apparently, the Lalas had too, because they both rushed in "to help me."

There was a table set with a pumpkin-and-apple pie and a bottle of beet juice and very fancy china.

We did, and it felt good to have a break from the house and all the creatures that lived in it. I felt a bit guilty about being THAT happy spending time away from my *Olgamuse*s, but then Mr. Hoopah came in with a potato-and-cheese cake that totally took my mind off all of my responsibilities.

CAKE IS A VERY EFFECTIVE GUILT ERASER.

After we ate lunch, we took time to look at all the photos of Mr. Hoopah on the wall. I had no idea he had led such an interesting life!

MR. HOOPAH
AS A CHILD WITH
HIS DOG.

MR. HOOPAH
RIDING A CAMEL IN
THE DESERT.

MR. HOOPAH
WITH A MARATHON
GOLD MEDAL.

MR. HOOPAH
ON TOP OF A
MOUNTAIN.

MR. HOOPAH
IN A **BOXING** MATCH.

MR. HOOPAH
IN A **CAVE** SURROUNDED
BY **BIG BATS.**

Mr. Hoopah had time to do all that stuff AND take care of his store 24/7?

I wanted to read about some of the places Mr. Hoopah had been, but instead, I came home to a giant mess. And a circus!

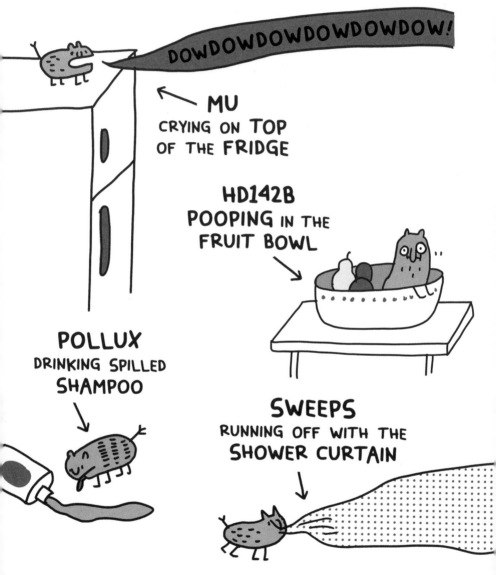

DOWDOWDOWDOWDOWDOW!

← MU
CRYING ON TOP
OF THE FRIDGE

HD142B
POOPING IN THE
FRUIT BOWL

POLLUX
DRINKING SPILLED
SHAMPOO

SWEEPS
RUNNING OFF WITH THE
SHOWER CURTAIN

I wondered what else had happened that I didn't see!

92

I was only one person, and there were seven *Olgamuses* running around! I was way too tired to take care of their messes, so I threw them all into the bathtub.

Just like their mom, the babies LOVE baths, and I ask you: What's cuter than a bathtub full of happy little furry creatures?

NOTHING.

After they were dry, I wrapped them all in a big fluffy blanket and carried them to my bed, where we all fell asleep almost instantly.

OBSERVATION #15:

HOW CAN ANYONE COMPLAIN ABOUT HER LIFE WHEN SHE'S IN THE MIDDLE OF A GIANT, FLUFFY CUDDLE?

6

CLEANING IS
MY LIFE NOW

I skipped a couple more days of entries because, as I said before, I'm pretty much a human washing machine now, and a human washing machine doesn't have much time for research.

TURN ME OFF

FROM TIME TO TIME

Here's a pie chart of my daily life these days:

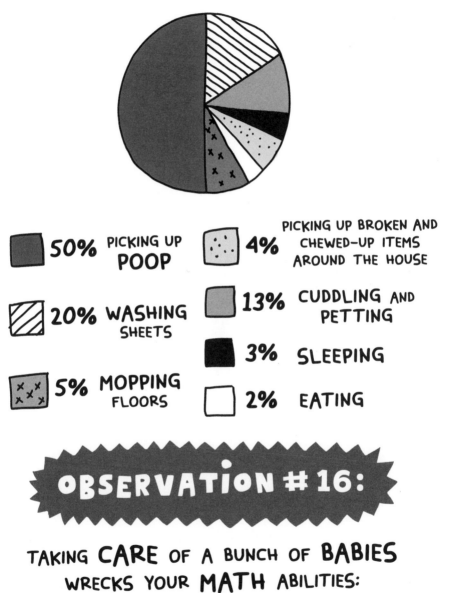

■ **50%** PICKING UP **POOP**	⬚ **4%** PICKING UP BROKEN AND CHEWED-UP ITEMS AROUND THE HOUSE
▨ **20%** WASHING SHEETS	■ **13%** CUDDLING AND PETTING
▨ **5%** MOPPING FLOORS	■ **3%** SLEEPING
	□ **2%** EATING

OBSERVATION #16:

TAKING **CARE** OF A BUNCH OF **BABIES**
WRECKS YOUR **MATH** ABILITIES:
I LEFT **3 PERCENT** OUT.

It's very hard to find time to write down all my discoveries about the babies. Here are some I made in the last few days about their emerging personalities:

HD142B IS THE ONE WHO LOOKS THE **MOST** LIKE HER **MAMA**. SHE'S CUDDLY, AND SHE **EATS** AND **SLEEPS** MOST OF THE TIME.

DOWDOWD DOWD!

POLLUX THINKS HE'S **VERY THREATENING.** HE'S THE ONE WHO HAS MASTERED THE **DOWDOWDOWD** THE BEST. I ALWAYS **PRETEND** TO BE **SCARED** WHEN HE TRIES IT, AND THEN HE LOOKS SO **PROUD!**

SWEEPS AND **DENIS** ARE VERY **TWINLIKE:** THEY LOOK SIMILAR AND THEY'RE **ALWAYS** TOGETHER. THEY ALSO **SLEEP** ON TOP OF EACH OTHER, WHICH IS **ADORABLE.**

UPSI IS VERY STRONG. SHE IS **TINY**, BUT SHE CAN **TEAR** MY HOUSE APART ALL BY HERSELF. SHE'S ALSO THE **SMARTEST**— SHE'S ALREADY LEARNED TO **OPEN** THE FRIDGE DOOR!

TINY & MIGHTY!

OGLE IS **QUIET** AND LIKES TO STAY ON MY **SHOULDER** WHENEVER POSSIBLE. SHE SOMETIMES **BITES** MY EAR, BUT I **DON'T MIND** IT THAT MUCH—IT DOESN'T HURT.

MU IS **STILL** NOT GETTING AS MUCH FOOD AS HIS BROTHERS AND SISTERS. THEY **DON'T** LET HIM, AND IT BREAKS MY HEART. HE SEEMS **WEAKER** THAN THE REST OF THE FAMILY, AND MEH ISN'T DOING **ANYTHING** ABOUT IT.

SHOULD I INTERVENE?

The postman brought me something today: the newest issue of *Awesome* magazine.

First of all, I look absolutely ridiculous on the cover with all that makeup. It's not me at all!

Secondly, they made a spelling mistake. Look!

They took the ONE piece of important information about Meh and managed to get it wrong. I rolled my eyes so hard I almost saw my brain.

Mistakes or not, the Lalas were going to love seeing it, so I thought I should go next door and show them.

They were more than thrilled: it was as if they had come face-to-face with Bip Bibop, their favorite Korean pop star.

I never knew the human voice could reach such a high pitch. They sounded more like seagulls than humans.

We called Chuck to show him too. He came, looked at the article, and laughed and laughed and laughed and laughed.

I hadn't really been all the way inside the Lalas' house, and I was surprised to realize how much I LOVED their place. First of all, it was so QUIET! And it smelled good too. Clean and perfumy, a very stark contrast to my own place (especially these days).

But I didn't stay there for too long. It's a weird feeling—I'm exhausted from taking care of my pets, but I can't stand being away from them either.

I THINK I SUFFER FROM
SEPARATION ANXIETY:

STAGE 1:
AFTER 5 MINUTES

STAGE 2:
AFTER 15 MINUTES

STAGE 3:
AFTER 1/2 HOUR

I'LL BE RIGHT BAAAACK!

When I got home, I compared my messy house to my neighbors' perfectly clean house, and it looked like a burglar had come in and had thrown everything he could find up in the air to see where it would land.

MEET THE CRAZY MESSY BURGLAR

I'd cleaned all day, gone out for two hours at the most, and here I was again.

OBSERVATION #18:

I THINK I'VE DISCOVERED A NEW SCIENTIFIC SOURCE OF **CONSTANT MOTION:** BABIES CREATE A **MESS** THAT I HAVE TO **CLEAN** UP. OVER AND OVER AND OVER.

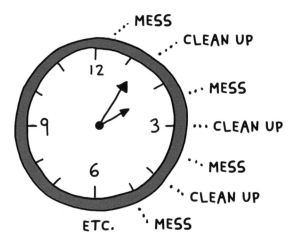

MESS
CLEAN UP
MESS
CLEAN UP
MESS
CLEAN UP
ETC. MESS

When I checked on the family, they were all in their garbage can, sleeping.

All but one.

Somehow Mu had gotten out of the garbage can and was sleeping alone on the rug. Had his own family kicked him out? Was he at least allowed to eat first?

The poor thing.

OBSERVATION #19:

I THOUGHT ONLY HUMANS COULD BE CRUEL, BUT IT SEEMS LIKE NATURE CAN BE TOO.

I took little Mu to bed with me so he wouldn't have to sleep alone. Tomorrow I'll find a way to get that hungry guy fed.

7

THE
RUNT

I didn't sleep a wink. The whole night I was afraid I'd roll over and crush poor Mu. Then at five thirty, we were ambushed by the rest of the *Olgamus* tribe. They came in, jumped on my bed, decided that it was the perfect time to destroy blankets, walked on my face, bit my feet and toes, and got into at least three wrestling matches on my stomach.

When they left, Meh jumped on the bed and snuggled next to me. This was the perfect time to give Mu his big chance, so I grabbed Mu and gently placed him next to Meh's tummy.

Within two seconds, all the babies were back! Upsi attacked Mu. She rammed right into the poor guy until he had to let go.

HEY! UPSI! THAT'S NOT VERY NICE. YOU HAVE TO TAKE TURNS!

He jumped onto the floor. Ouch! Now he was chewing on my foot!

OBSERVATION # 20:

OLGAMUS TEETH AND HUMAN FEET ARE **NOT** MEANT TO GO TOGETHER.

Compared to the others, Mu seemed so small and weak. But how could I make them understand? They were just babies, and I was discovering that babies don't know the first thing about sharing.

After stepping in another pile of *Olgamus* poop, I noticed the awful state of my room and felt like I might cry. It was such a mess, and I was soooo tired.

I needed a break, and I needed a quiet place to do some research about what to do when a baby won't eat!

Ms. Swoop told me that if I came to the library, I could pick up a few comic books. I packed my things, kissed each *Olgamus*, and left.

When I opened my front door, there were a million flashes!

There were others, too. I ran as fast as I could to get away from them. I might be tiny, but I'm a fast runner, and the reporters with their heavy cameras were not.

I finally made it to the library.

I sat down at the computer and started looking up information about baby animals.

OBSERVATION # 21:

WHEN YOU DO RESEARCH ONLINE,
IT'S EASY TO GET LOST IN MOUNTAINS
OF USELESS STUFF.

SILLY PHOTOS

MORE ADS

FAKE NEWS

MEMES

ADS

CLICK BAIT

QUIZZES

CELEBRITIES

PEOPLE ARGUING

Here's what I found out about baby animals.

A BABY **SHARK** IS CALLED A **PUP.**

SOME **FROG** BABIES ARE BORN FROM **HOLES** IN THEIR **MOM'S BACK.**

SOME **BABY** SPIDERS **EAT** THEIR **MOTHERS** AFTER THEY ARE BORN. (I BETTER WARN RITA **NOT** TO HAVE KIDS!)

WOLF PUPS ARE
BORN COMPLETELY
BLIND AND DEAF.

WHEN A FEMALE **GIRAFFE**
GIVES BIRTH, THE BABY
CAN DROP **SIX** FEET
TO THE GROUND—BUT
IS ABLE TO **STAND** UP,
WALK, AND EVEN **RUN**
SHORTLY AFTERWARD.

ELEPHANT BABIES SUCK ON THEIR
OWN **TRUNKS** FOR **COMFORT**.

I know, this information isn't going to help me with Mu, but I can't help it. I love discovering these funny facts! I'm a curious girl.

I was hoping to be home by lunchtime to check on the family, but it was already way past lunch! Time was running out.

At last! I found a dog-breeding website called Paw Wow. They had information about all sorts of puppy problems, and then I found this. It was not good news!

PAW WOW

NIPPLE GUARDING

IF A SMALL PUPPY IS BORN INTO A LARGE LITTER, THE BIGGER AND STRONGER ONES WILL FIND THE BEST MILK-PRODUCING NIPPLE AND "GUARD" IT AND EVEN PREVENT THE SMALLER PUPPY (CALLED THE RUNT) FROM NURSING. THIS CAN LEAD TO MALNOURISHMENT AND EVEN DEATH.

DEATH?? Was my little Mu's life in danger? He was the runt!

According to the website, I had to help Mu by making sure he had some alone time with Meh. But how could I do this with all the other babies in the house?

I'd better figure it out quickly.

Maybe Chuck could help.

8

AN
EXPERIMENT

Chuck listened to my problem and had an idea instantaneously.

He went into the basement and came back with something that looked like a cage.

THIS IS MISTER'S CRATE. I USE IT WHEN I LEAVE THE HOUSE AND I DON'T WANT MISTER TO DESTROY EVERYTHING WHILE I'M GONE. IT'S HIS SPECIAL COZY PLACE. YOU SHOULD TRY PUTTING MEH IN HERE SO MU CAN NURSE IN PEACE.

That was an EXCELLENT idea. I hugged Chuck like he'd just saved my life.

EVERYONE NEEDS A SMART FRIEND IN THEIR LIFE.

We ran home with the crate and were welcomed by an *OLGAMUS* PARTY.

Upsi was rolling around on my skateboard; Ogle was unrolling toilet paper all over the floor, and Pollux was hanging from the kitchen lamp.

Meh came and rubbed against my legs. She looked tired and I could see why. I was exhausted after just two minutes in the house with her babies, and she spent 24/7 with them.

Chuck and I found Mu curled up on my pillow. He didn't look up when I called him. He looked asleep.

Chuck picked up Meh and put her in the crate. She didn't understand what was going on. I'd never, ever put her in one of those before. The only time she had been in anything like a cage was when she'd been at the vet before the babies were born, and I know she didn't have fond memories of that day.

Then I picked Mu up. He looked and felt like a deflated water balloon. He probably weighed the same too.

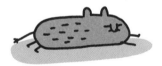

The poor little guy barely opened his eyes—and then he didn't react when I laid him next to Meh, who began licking him. Maybe she was trying to wake him up.

It didn't work.

When Chuck closed the little door, the other babies didn't like it one bit. They started climbing onto the cage, making their absurdly cute DOWDOWDOWD cries. They wanted in.

Everything was getting worse! All the *Olgamuses* were in distress, and Mu wasn't waking up to nurse. Our plan wasn't working. I felt like crying.

WE NEED A WAY TO **DISTRACT** THE BABIES! I'LL GO GET THE **LALAS**.

While Chuck was gone, I picked up the other babies myself and took them to my bedroom, where they began complaining. I closed the door behind me so that Mu and Meh would have some quiet time to nurse. But Mu was sleeping, not eating.

COME ON, BABY, COME ON, COME ON! WAKE UP!

Chuck came back with the Lalas, who were very worried.

But hand-feed him what? On the website, they said to feed puppies milk formula, but I have no clue if dog milk and *Olgamus* milk are the same thing. Not all mammals' milks are exactly the same. I don't want to poison the poor little guy!

MAYBE WE SHOULD **LOOK** AT MEH'S MILK UNDER THE **MICROSCOPE** AND SEE WHAT IT'S **MADE** OF!

THAT'S A **GOOD IDEA**, ACTUALLY, ALTHOUGH A BIT MESSY. CAN YOU GET A **DROP** OF **MILK** FROM MEH? I'LL GET MY MICROSCOPE.

EWWW! ARE YOU **CRAZY?**

Oh, yeah. The Lalas are disgusted by almost anything. So I got the drop of milk from Meh (no, I don't need to illustrate this) and Chuck got the microscope.

I LOVE looking at things under the microscope. Here are things I've observed before:

FINGERNAILS

SNOWFLAKES

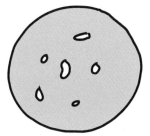

PLANT LEAVES

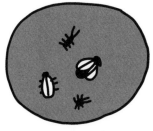

BOOGERS (OH STOP IT, IT'S **FUN!**)

DEAD BUGS (WHO DIED **NATURAL** DEATHS, OF COURSE)

AMAZING SCIENTIFIC MOMENT!

This was the first time any scientist had ever looked at *Olgamus* milk. I carefully set the drop of milk on a glass slide, adjusted the lenses, and took a look.

Here is what we saw:

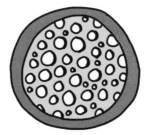

It didn't give us a list of ingredients.

I felt sorry for ever thinking that the Lalas were silly or dumb. They have pretty good ideas. A milk and olive oil formula might not be the solution to Mu's problem, but it was certainly worth trying.

I didn't have olive oil at home, but the Lalas did: they said they used it in their DIY beauty products.

Here's the recipe we used:

3 PARTS OLIVE OIL

1 PART MILK

MIX IN A BABY BOTTLE AND SHAKE WELL

HEAT UP IN A POT OF WATER

While Farla was playing with the babies in the bedroom and trying to keep them quiet, I picked up Mu from the crate. Chuck and Shalala stayed with Meh. She fretted whenever someone picked up one of her babies.

I sat down with Mu on the couch, cradling him in one arm like a human baby. He was still sleeping, so I opened his little mouth myself and put the bottle right in.

At first, he had no reaction. But then he started suckling. It seemed he was barely able to get anything, but when I looked at the bottle again and saw the milk going down, I knew it was working!

Mu drank about a quarter of the bottle and closed his eyes. There was no way to wake him up for more—he was out cold—so I set him up on a cushion and let him sleep.

I woke up to the awful sound of howling. There was a beast jumping on my legs. I turned over and tried to fall back asleep, but Upsi wasn't letting me.

I tried to grab Upsi but couldn't catch her. I looked up, but guess what. It wasn't Upsi jumping on my legs—it was Mu! Mu, looking healthy and very energetic! And HUNGRY.

THE BRAND-NEW MU

I set Mu up next to his mama, and just like that—he started eating right away. Meh started purring. She seemed relieved.

RRR
RRRR
RRRRR

VICTORY!

The milky olive formula we'd made had worked.

Hey, guys! Yippee! All the pups came running up and jumped on me. I fell down, and we rolled around on the carpet.

I played with each one of the babies. I was so happy that everyone was feeling good! I celebrated by making myself some mac and cheese with pickles.

OBSERVATION # 23:

MAC AND CHEESE IS **BETTER** THAN CAKE FOR CELEBRATION PURPOSES.

I had to tell my friends the great news about Mu. I knocked on the Lalas' door and told them everything. They wanted to come with me to tell Chuck, Mr. Hoopah, and Ms. Swoop.

I FELT LIKE HANDING OUT FLYERS.

EXTRA! EXTRA! READ ALL ABOUT MU'S RECOVERY!

Everybody was as relieved as I was. Ms. Swoop gave me a book she had found on how to train puppies to do tricks. I decided I'd try to train the *Olgamuses* as soon as I got a chance.

THINGS I MIGHT TRAIN THE *OLGAMUSES* TO DO:

BRING ME MY
SLIPPERS
(OF COURSE,
IT'S A CLASSIC)

IRISH DANCE

TIPPITY TAP

MAKE MY
BED

Mr. Hoopah and Ms. Swoop hadn't met the babies yet, so I invited everybody to come back to my place.

When I opened the door, the smell was THORRIBLE (it's a word I made up to express something that's terrible and horrible at the same time). It smelled like a pack of pigs living inside a garbage truck on the hottest day in August.

And that wasn't even the worst part.

The babies had kicked my microscope off the desk and dug a hole inside my couch. My microscope was smashed to pieces!

This was too much. I loved my microscope and I was very SMAD (that's mad and sad at the same time. Okay, I'll stop that now).

How can they be so adorable one second and so destructive the next?

That was brilliant. I thought I'd seen leashes and collars at Mr. Hoopah's store.

We all went together and bought eight leashes plus collars. It cost me $24, but hey, if that's the price for mental health, it's worth it.

Then the real fun began.

It took us forty-five minutes just to get the little beasts into their little collars.

TUTORIAL:
HOW TO PUT A LEASH ON AN
OLGAMUS IN 37 EASY STEPS

1. TRY TO CATCH **ONE.**

2. RETRIEVE HIM FROM **UNDER** THE **COUCH.**

3. TRY TO KEEP HIM IMMOBILE.

4. TRY SOME MORE.

OW!

5. GRAB THE COLLAR WITH ONE HAND.

6. RETRIEVE THE ESCAPEE FROM TOP OF FRIDGE.

7. SQUEEZE HIM BETWEEN YOUR KNEES.

8. AVOID HIS SHARP TEETH.

OW!

9. BUCKLE THE COLLAR AS **FAST** AS YOU POSSIBLY CAN.

10. REPEAT AS MANY TIMES AS NEEDED WITH **OTHER** *OLGAMUS*ES.

OBSERVATION # 24:

I'M PRETTY SURE IT WOULD BE **EASIER** TO PUT A COLLAR ON A HYSTERICAL T. REX.

Here's a picture of us after we had finally managed to get the collars on.

I don't know how we finally got to the dog park, but we made it, and everyone was still alive.

OBSERVATION # 25:

BABY *OLGAMUSES* ARE **NOT** BORN WITH THE **ABILITY** TO FOLLOW **HUMANS**.

Once we got there and set them free, it was HAPPI-NESS AT FIRST SIGHT.

It was the best afternoon I've had in a long time. I could have sat there forever watching my *Olgamus* friends being healthy and happy.

WE NEED **MORE** DAYS LIKE THIS, MEH. BUT WE **CAN'T** DO **EVERYTHING** BY OURSELVES. WE NEED HELP. **LOTS** OF **HELP.**

10

THE
PACKAGE

When we got home from the park, a surprise was waiting on the front porch: this GINORMOUS BOX.

I have to admit that I'm a huge package fan too.

OBSERVATION # 26:

IS THERE **ANYTHING** COOLER THAN GETTING PRESENTS IN THE **MAIL**?

There was no indication of what was inside the box, so I was a bit wary. What if it was a prank? Or a bunch of annoying paparazzi trying to take photos of us?

I looked at the return address on the package:

The Lalas started jumping up and down next to me.

WHAT IF IT'S A WHOLE BUNCH OF **MAKEUP?**

OR A NEW **WARDROBE?** OPEN IT! OPEN IT! OPEN IT!

First I wrangled all the *Olgamuse*s and brought them inside. Then we all dragged the extremely heavy box into the living room. What could it BE?

I started prying the top open.

Out came a bunch of those foamy peanut thingies that they use for packing fragile stuff. We took those out and put them on the floor. The *Olgamuses* went crazy! They were running around the pile as if it were Christmas and they were playing in the snow.

Here's what was in the box:

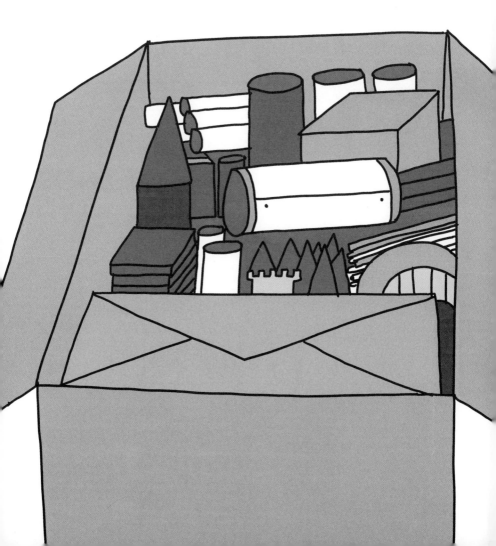

"Look!" said Chuck. "There's a note."

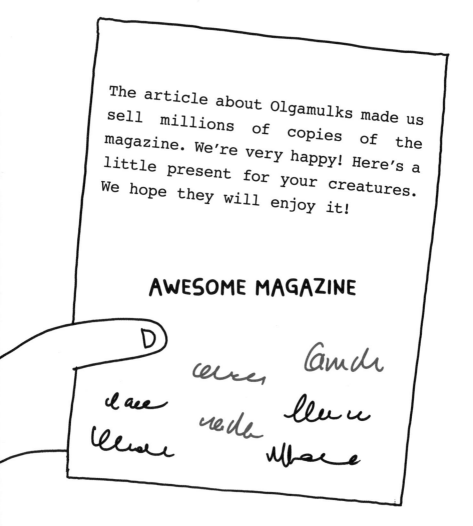

The article about Olgamulks made us sell millions of copies of the magazine. We're very happy! Here's a little present for your creatures. We hope they will enjoy it!

AWESOME MAGAZINE

I still had no clue what it was! The Lalas, Chuck, and I started unpacking it, piece by piece. Soon the living room was full of nuts, bolts, tubes, springs, pipes, and all sorts of things.

"Oh, I get it!" said Chuck. "It's a pet house! I found the instruction booklet!"

This was so cool. I just LOVE putting stuff together.

We all got to work. The Lalas were pretty good at figuring out complicated stuff, while Chuck was creative with the parts he found, transforming roofs into bathtubs and doors into windows.

After a few hours of headaches, lost screws, and unidentifiable parts, we finally finished it.

We put Sweeps and Denis in the house first, but they seemed more interested in the foamy peanuts. So I tried Meh.

She just sat there.

We tried again with the other babies. At first, they didn't seem to know what to do, but after a few minutes, the fun began.

This was a great gift. I have to send a thank-you note to the people at *Awesome* magazine.

The *Olgamus* house thingy was huge! It took up most of the living room, but I can't complain! I knew my life would change when I decided to adopt an alien.

Plus, watching the happy little animals was fun.

OBSERVATION # 27:

PET HOUSES ARE **BETTER** THAN TV.

THANK YOU, AWESOME!
OLGA xox

Lots of stuff has happened since my last entry; I had to take a break to reflect on my life with the *Olgamuse*s.

As much as I adore the babies, being an alien zookeeper/grandma/caregiver has turned out to be too much for one person.

Besides, my house is too small for seven extra-energetic, fast-growing creatures and their mother. And when I say "fast-growing," I'm not kidding. Here's their growth chart since they were born.

NAME	BIRTH	NOW
UPSI	1/4 POUND	3 POUNDS
MU	1/4 POUND	6 POUNDS
OGLE	1/2 POUND	5.5 POUNDS
POLLUX	1/2 POUND	4 POUNDS
SWEEPS	1/3 POUND	3.5 POUNDS
DENIS	1/3 POUND	4.5 POUNDS
HD142B	1/3 POUND	5.5 POUNDS

Yes, it's true. Mu is now the biggest of them all. If he keeps growing at this rate, he'll need to sleep in a dumpster instead of a garbage can.

Those aren't the only challenges. Pollux has grown some very long, silky pink hair. He looks like a mop now.

Also: Their skin has become totally opaque, like their mother's, so I can't see their insides anymore. But I have proof that their digestive system is in tiptop shape.

OBSERVATION # 28:

I REALLY HAVE TO DO SOME RESEARCH ON ECOLOGICAL WAYS TO USE THEIR **POOP.**

ENERGY?
I READ THAT SOME **COUNTRIES** HAVE FIGURED OUT WAYS TO USE **WASTE** AS AN ENERGY SOURCE.

COMPOST FOR A GARDEN?
(I DON'T HAVE A GARDEN! **YET!**)

Some grown-ups have complained that I use the word "poop" too much in my science notebooks, so I won't go into the proof I have about their digestive system, other than to say it looks like multicolored skittles, smells awful, and now comes in quantities that would make you dizzy.

Another milestone: The babies eat solid foods: mostly olives, of course. They almost don't nurse anymore, which is a relief to Meh, but now they eat like teenagers. Especially Mu.

Now for the math lovers out there, here's a fun question:

If Meh, when she was alone here, ate three jars of olives a week, how many jars a week will she and seven strapping teenage *Olgamus*es eat?*

AND I'M **NOT** RICH, YOU KNOW. OLIVES ARE **EXPENSIVE.**

*Answer: Around 24 jars a week! Yikes!

I realized quickly that I don't have the money, the time, the physical or mental strength—and the room I would need—to keep all the babies with me. And there is no way I'll be able to walk them all to the park every day by myself.

OBSERVATION # 29:

I'M **NOT** AN **OCTOPUS.**

OLGACTOPUS

I had to do something! (That's when I remembered!)

It was a very hard decision to make, but I had to consider it.

So I called all my friends—kids and grown-ups. I asked them if they would like to adopt one of the *Olgamuses*.

And guess what? ALL my friends said yes!

The Lalas were so excited they hugged me.

They chose two babies: Sweeps and Denis, who can't be separated anyway: they are always together.

INSEPARABLE

OLGAMUS TWINS

Chuck wanted one too. He knows that Mister gets along with most *Olgamus*es. He picked HD142B because she reminds him of Meh. Since Mister and Meh are very good friends, he thinks they'll like each other too.

A NEW FRIENSHIP IS BORN

Mr. Hoopah asked if he could have one to keep him company at the store. He gets lonely during his long evening shifts. I told him yes, and he picked Pollux, who can also serve as a guard *Olgamus*.

DOWDOWD?

AHEM, I'LL BE RIGHT BACK!

Ms. Swoop chose Ogle because she likes her peace and quiet. She wants to try to train Ogle to sit nicely on her shoulder at the library.

That left me with Meh, Mu, and Upsi. Three *Olgamus*es and me. A happy family of four. That was still a big number of *Olgamus*es, so I got to keep the *Olgamus* house.

Still, giving away more than half my *Olgamus* family was breaking my heart. There was no way I'd let them go without being sure I'd see them all the time. I trust my human friends, but I needed to be completely sure, so I made them all sign this contract:

I PROMISE TO ACCOMPANY OLGA AND HER PETS TO THE DOG PARK AT LEAST ONCE A WEEK AND TO PROVIDE HER WITH A DETAILED REPORT ON THEIR HEALTH, GROWTH, AND BEHAVIOR FROM TIME TO TIME.

CHUCK

Ed Hoopah

Farla Lala

Nathalie Swoop xox

Shalala Lala ♥

I had one last group hug with my favorite creatures, and then I hugged the kind humans who would soon be taking care of them. I know my aliens are in good hands and that together we make one big, loving, human-*Olgamus* family.

GROUP HUG!

I feel so lucky as a scientist. First of all, I made the coolest discovery of all time (in my opinion), but in the process, I also:

MADE **LOTS** OF FRIENDS

RESTORED MY **FAITH** IN **HUMANITY**

LEARNED WHAT **TRUE LOVE** IS.

Thank you, *Olgamuses*.

HOW TO DRAW AN

OLGAMUS

 DRAW THE EARS

 DRAW THE BODY

← WIDER AT THE BACK

3 **ADD THE FACE . . . AND THE REST**

AND **NOW,** YOU CAN **PERSONALIZE** YOUR **OLGAMUS** AND MAKE IT

UNIQUE!

ADD **PATTERNS**

OR **HAIR**   OR **ACCESSORIES**

OR MAKE IT **UNIQUE** IN ITS OWN WAY!

AND **OF COURSE,** GIVE IT A **NAME!**

WOULDN'T IT BE **FUN** IF WE COULD SEE **INSIDE** THE BODIES OF OTHER CREATURES? UNTIL **X-RAY GOGGLES** EXIST, HERE ARE **DRAWINGS** OF THE INSIDES OF SOME ANIMALS:

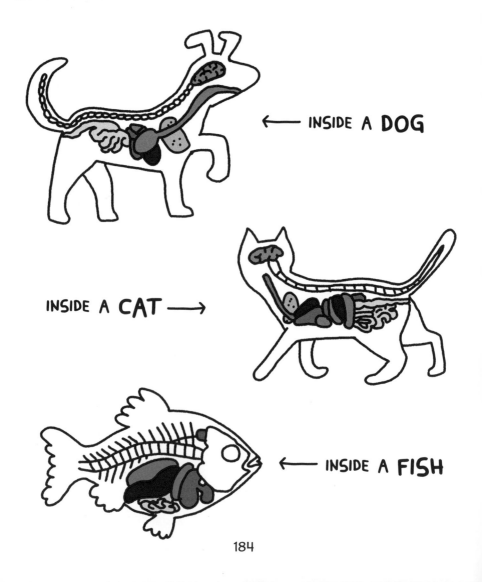

← INSIDE A **DOG**

INSIDE A **CAT** →

← INSIDE A **FISH**

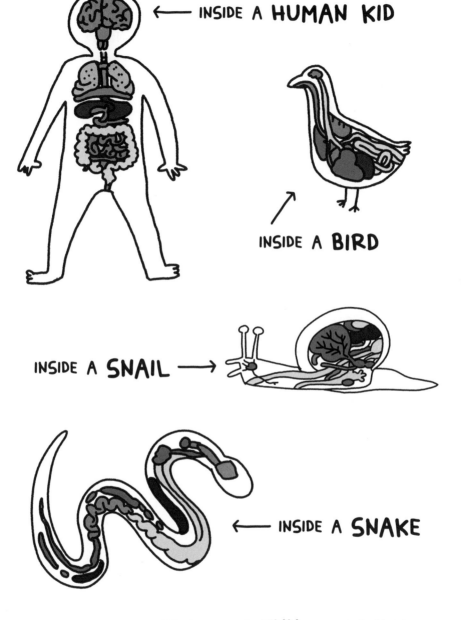

INSIDE A **HUMAN KID**

INSIDE A **BIRD**

INSIDE A **SNAIL** →

← INSIDE A **SNAKE**

THESE DRAWINGS ARE FOR **FUN.** WOULD YOU
LIKE TO KNOW **MORE** ABOUT WHAT'S INSIDE
ANIMALS AND HUMANS? ASK YOUR **LIBRARIAN**
ABOUT **BOOKS** ON **ANATOMY!**